Yesterday's Shadows

six short stories from the past

David R. Beshears

Large Print Edition

Greybeard Publishing
Washington State

Greybeard Publishing
P.O. Box 480
McCleary, WA 98557-0480

The stories included in this novella
have previously been offered in
different formats and media.

This is the first time all have been
published together under the
"Yesterday's Shadows" collection title.

ISBN: 978-0-9961818-5-3
(large print edition)

A word from the author...

Six short stories from the past...

I don't get to write short stories much anymore, but I do love writing them. Short stories was where I started, back when I was twelve and my sixth grade teacher handed me an empty theme book and asked me to fill it up. I had turned in a story the day before for extra credit and she liked it.

Most of my short stories have been lost, particularly those written using my old typewriter back before I had a computer, and more than a few written with only pencil and paper. But I did manage to hang onto a couple from way back when.

I thought I'd bring some of these old stories out into the light. I hope you like 'em.

-drb

Update 2019

Yesterday's Shadows, Reunions, Room and The Light in the Mist have all been adapted to short script screenplays, and in each case have been expanded and modified to fit the format. All these short scripts are being marketed to independent film producers.

The Last Day at Sharp Park story was used as the "seed" for a pilot episode script of a series titled "Miles Bennett". This pilot episode screenplay was then adapted to a novella. Note that the novella has little in common with the short story in this collection beyond the core concept of an elderly woman and her grandson in hiding.

Table of Contents

Yesterday's Shadows

Introduction

This was written sometime around 1975, so I was about eighteen or nineteen years old at the time. It begins as an Outer Limits kind of post-disaster tale and then takes a left turn into the Twilight Zone. I'm certain I had no idea of the influence of these programs at the time I was writing it, but in reading it now, that influence is obvious.

Yesterday's Shadows

The sun would be setting soon. Time to find a place to spend the night.

Peter took his steps cautiously, walking down the center of the street, carefully examining each house that he passed. They stared back emptily, their windows dull and gray; most had their curtains drawn.

There were no sounds but that of his own footsteps echoing out ahead of him.

He watched for any sign of movement, anything to show that his presence had caught someone's attention. Anything... a shadow falling across a window, a door slowly and silently closing, a curtain falling back into place. But there was nothing. If there was anyone here, they were too weak or too frightened to show themselves, even guardedly. If anyone watched, hidden away in the dark, from behind those dark, dusty drapes, they would rather this man pass by, leave them alone to their few remaining days.

Slow and steady. Walk with confidence. You are strong and healthy and unafraid. You can take on anything and anyone...

What the hell am I doing out in the middle of the street?

Gotta find a place for the night...

Peter stepped onto the sidewalk and stopped in front of the very next house. This would do. A nice little place. Pleasant, modest, warm atmosphere. Brown stucco. He liked the short hedge that lined the walk leading up to the porch. The lawn was dry and showing signs of neglect, but that was to be expected, wasn't it? What with everything that had happened over the last six months.

Peter walked up to the front door as if he owned the place. The sun, low on the horizon, moved from behind a narrow band of clouds and shown on the door and the large front window.

He turned with a final glance up and down the street, at the windows of the row of houses that faced this one. Not a creature was stirring...

The door was locked. He stepped off the porch and walked around to the side of the house, was about to break a window when he found one unlocked.

He climbed into the bedroom that had belonged to a young boy. There was a cute bedspread, about a hundred toys sitting on plastic shelves, almost as many more strewn about on the floor. There were little-boy clothes on the floor beside the bed, and posters hanging on the walls advertised fantasy movies that had premiered long before the little boy was born.

Peter stopped in the hallway, felt for the bulge in the pocket of his jacket. He had quit carrying the rifle several months ago, but had decided to keep the pistol. In all the time he had carried the rifle, he had only fired it once, and he had missed.

True, he had been in situations where perhaps someone else might have used it, but he hadn't been able to bring himself to kill someone as desperate as those that he had come across. If it actually came down to *him or me*, he had no doubts about what he could do, but up to now he had always been able to back out of such situations gracefully. Finally, one day, he just didn't pick up the rifle when he moved on and had yet to have cause to get another one.

Peter let the small backpack slip down to the floor, pulled the pistol from his pocket, let his arms hang loose at his sides. He searched the other bedrooms and bathroom. He noticed the bed in the master bedroom wasn't made. The odor in the bathroom told him that someone had used the toilet after the plumbing had gone out, and he quickly closed the door.

He closed the bedroom doors as he walked back towards the front of the house. The living room looked neat and orderly. The drapes at the windows were thin and let in what little sunlight remained. Several books and magazines were set out on the coffee table and end tables.

"Honey," he called out cynically. "I'm home..."

Stepping into the kitchen, he stopped abruptly, in mid-stride and took a half-step back. His heart seemed to hold its last beat; his breath caught in his throat.

"Hello, *dear*," said the woman.

It took several moments, but Peter managed to let go the breath, if somewhat shakily.

"Hi," he said.

The woman was sitting at the kitchen table, sipping something out of a coffee cup. She wasn't looking at Peter, but staring off into space as if in thought.

"Who are you?" he finally managed to ask. *A stupid thing to ask...*

The woman set the cup down onto the saucer. It gave off a light *chink* sound. She turned her head then and looked at Peter. For several long moments she stared silently. He began to think she wasn't going to say anything.

"Anna," she said at last. She lifted a brow. "Who are you?"

Peter realized that he was still holding the pistol. He quickly stuffed it back into his jacket pocket. "Peter," he said clumsily. "I'm Peter."

"Have a seat, Peter." Anna picked up the coffee cup. She was trying a little too hard at this *family in the suburbs* thing.

Peter walked over to the counter and leaned against it. "This your house?"

"I was here before you."

Peter shrugged. "Okay... I guess I can find somewhere else to stay."

"Yes," she said stiffly. "I shouldn't think that would be too difficult."

The warm welcome of a few moments before had now hit a definite sour note. Was she intentionally trying to keep him off balance? It wouldn't be hard to do, and he certainly couldn't blame her. Someone in her position, in times like these, could fall prey to any number of dangers. When she looked up at him, an intensity in her eyes forced Peter to turn away. The cupboard doors were inset with glass panes, and he could see the dishes and canned goods inside.

"I suppose not," he said. Looking side-glance, and then turning back again, he watched her carefully set the cup down. She was probably in her late twenties, maybe thirty. She had thick, dark hair, combed and neat. She wore clean jeans and a heavy shirt. Hard to tell, but Peter suspected that she had a nice figure. Her face was attractive, and she still had a healthy look about her. He sensed that she knew he was staring and so turned to look out the window.

Anna brought her elbows up onto the table and rested her chin in one cupped palm. "I have several jugs of water in the cupboard there behind you," she said. "There's some drink mix in the other."

"Thanks." Peter was glad of the opportunity to do something other than stand about looking like an idiot. Even so, he almost dropped the plastic jug and managed to spill as much iced tea mix onto the counter as he put into the glass. Anna opened a can of peaches and served up two bowls, set them on the table. The cupboards were well stocked with a wide variety of canned and boxed foods, which meant that Anna probably planned on staying for a while.

They ate quietly for several minutes, each glancing at the other when one thought the other wasn't looking. Peter finished off his bowl of fruit, set it aside and took another long drink of the tea.

"Have you been here long?" he asked.

"A couple of weeks."

"And you plan on staying," he stated flatly.

"Plan on it, yes."

Peter looked into her eyes and managed this time not to turn away. "What stage are you in?" he asked her.

"Rather blunt," she said. "Six. Maybe Five by now. I'm not sure."

"Can't be Five. There'd be more sign."

"It's hard to tell when you're alone. You can't trust what you see or feel."

"I've had a few doubts."

Anna leaned back in her chair. She seemed a little more comfortable than before. As for himself, Peter saw the mist clearing. He called it the *mist*. When you are alone, there is a hum in the silence that forms a mist in your mind. Only another human voice can burn it away. Anna's voice was soft and he liked the sound of it.

"You can't be more than Stage Seven," she said.

"Coming on Six soon, I think."

Anna nodded slowly; the gray haunt of her eyes grew more shadowed, filmy. "Not many left at Seven."

"Just me," he agreed.

"Do you realize that by the time you reach Stage One, you'll probably be the only person left alive?" she asked. "On the whole planet..."

Pleasant kitchen table conversation, thought Peter. *Yes, he did realize that...*

"That makes you kind of special, don't you think?" Anna leaned forward, reached out, almost took Peter's hand, but stopped just short. She stared absently at her own. "You'll be the last man on Earth. The very last. Then... after that..." Her voice went dead.

Peter pulled back, stood and nervously put his bowl in the sink. *Does she wash the dishes or just throw them out into the yard?*

"I'm sure there are healthy people out there," he said. "Somewhere. Some people are probably immune. And I'm sure some of the important people managed to hide away somewhere safe."

"No one got away," she said. "No one knew it was here until it was too late. Oh, they hid away once they realized how serious it really was, but by then we had all been breathing it in for weeks, or months. No one knew about it. No one suspected." She paused and the silence hurt. Peter came back to the table and sat down, hands folded in his lap. When Anna spoke again, she was vague and distant. She had probably said all this to herself a thousand times before. There would have been no one else around to listen. "Animals started dying, people started dying, and everyone said, *'my, my, what could it be?'*, and then more people died and then everyone started pointing fingers, saying *'it's his fault'* or *'it's their fault'*. And more people died. Then a few stood up, looked around and said *'my, my, look at how many people have died'*."

Her voice had gone low and soft, until Peter could hardly hear her, until it faded and finally died. They sat in silence.

"No one is immune," she said suddenly. "It's in all of us and we are all going to die. There are doctors out there, still alive, still working on it, but they've only been at it a couple of months, and even if they are only at Stage Seven, like you, they only have a couple of months left. Like you. When they die, whatever little they have managed to learn will go with them. But that won't matter. Because there won't be anyone left to pick up where they left off. No one left to save."

He knew that she was probably right. Just a few weeks earlier, he had been near Los Angeles. The stench wouldn't let him get any nearer than a few miles. At one time, bodies were gathered and burned, but not anymore. There were too many dead and not enough living. Besides, those still alive weren't worried about disease. They would be gone themselves, soon enough. Out of respect or a promise, a husband may bury his wife, or a child his mother, but there were millions, billions, of bodies out there.

"Do you think there's life on other planets?" she asked suddenly.

"What?"

"I hope there's life on other planets." She paused then, again. She grew distant, again. She wasn't waiting for a response from Peter. She wasn't listening for anything that might be spoken in this kitchen. Her face had a vague, faraway look. "I would hate to think that all the life in the universe was here on this planet. That would mean that when the last of us dies, when you die, then the universe will be empty."

Peter leaned forward, "Anna, I—"

"If there is no one left to witness the universe's existence, it's just... here."

"I'm sure there is—"

"How said that would be."

"We can't be all there is."

There was a long, uncomfortable silence.

"I hope not," she said.

"I'm sure we're not..." Peter said softly.

A sound then, a faint sound, distant, coming out of the past... a child's playful giggle.

Peter stood again, stepped slowly to the open arch leading to the rest of the house. He leaned against the frame, looked into the living room...

Slowly coming into the focus...

A five year old boy runs down the hallway, a bright grin on his happy face. He runs into the living room, table lamps aglow. He rushes to a young man sitting in the chair reading a magazine. The boy leaps into his Daddy's lap just as the man lifts the magazine safely aside.

A young woman sitting on the couch lowers the magazine she's been reading, smiles and watches the scene.

Fading then to...

The living room, now gray, the only light coming through faded curtains. The woman is standing in the middle of the room, her arms wrapped about herself, her expression as gray as the room.

The man comes into the living room from the hallway, the little boy in his arms, wrapped in a super-hero blanket, his little head lying tiredly on Daddy's shoulders.

Mom and Dad look at each other, distraught, desperation edging to surrender. They turn toward the front door, the woman picking up a small suitcase on their way out...

Peter turned away from the opening, worked his way back into the kitchen, sat at the table. He smiled awkwardly, slightly embarrassed as he wiped at his cheek.

A little damp perhaps, but no tears.

Anna gave a knowing smile.

"No tears left?"

"Oh, I don't know about that," he said, a clumsy grin. "I still shed a few, now and then. I'm usually alone, though."

"Well that's just depressing."

"Comes with the way of things."

Anna looked away, then. "Alone is wrong. Tears alone is wrong. Facing the end alone... is very wrong."

"There's been a lot of wrong lately."

"A lot of alone. Too much alone." She fought back tears of her own. She managed to look back across the table. "I don't want to be alone, Peter."

Peter leaned across the table, reached out and took Anna's hands into his own.

"You won't be," he said. "I'm here. If you want me."

Feelings for this woman welled up inside him until he could hardly breathe. He felt dizzy, heady.

Where was this coming from? He wondered. Was it some sort of *Last Man and Woman* thing?

Would he have felt this way if it had been someone else that he had found in this kitchen?

Confusing thoughts—muddled, confusing thoughts...

Is this another symptom?

Anna smiled sadly.

"And what about you?" she asked. "You'll be all alone, after I..."

"Right now, I'm looking at today," he stated firmly. "Let's live today. When tomorrow comes, we'll live tomorrow."

"Yes," said Anna. "I like that."

Peter moved slowly across the kitchen and sat at the table. He reached across and spoke gentle, loving words, laughed lightly at a response that may have been whispered as if into his ear alone. Sitting back, his arms brushed at the heavy layer of dust that covered the table. The kitchen was gray and dingy, and the dust covered everything. A cup and saucer rested on the table in front of an empty chair, abandoned long ago. The inside of the cup was stained from a remaining swallow of coffee that had been left behind and evaporated away months earlier. The rim of the cup was chipped. Pointing to the cup now, Peter asked his companion if she would like a refill. Looking to the empty chair, he listened to her response, stood and walked over to the counter, talking over his shoulder as he opened the cupboard. There was a single can of peaches, an empty jar of instant iced tea mix, and three packets of Kool-Aid.

Glancing once at the sink, he wondered again whether she washed her dishes or simply tossed them out the kitchen window and into the yard.

Laughing at something Anna said, Peter almost dropped the jar of tea mix that he was taking from the well-stocked cupboard. He smiled as he looked back at her. The more she opened up to him, the more he realized just how wonderful she was. The more he realized just how much he needed her. He would do his best to make her happy in the few months she had left. Together, they would share their joys as well as their fears.

Peter would see that Anna was never alone again.

No one should have to be alone...

~ end

Reunions

Introduction

"Reunions" was first published in Necrology Magazine, Tales of Macabre and Horror, a publication tending toward the H.P. Lovecraft type of dark story. Someone suggested that I write an offbeat horror tale, and this little story was the result.

Reunions

Mrs. Johansen held tightly to the handles of the walker and pushed it through the door, following carefully along behind it as she came into the small dining hall. The others were already there, sitting at the one, round table situated in the middle of the room; Mr. Borden, Miss Margaret, Old

Mason. They turned about as she came in. Familiar faces from out of the past. Mr. Borden stood and bowed his head in greeting. Mrs. Johansen smiled briefly in response and continued her way to the table.

Old Mason pulled out a chair for her. She stood beside it, shuffled to turn herself around and into position. Her shallow breaths shuddered past aged, trembling lips. She struggled to balance herself, one hand on the walker and the other held in the air above the handle, readying herself to reach for the back of the chair. Old Mason held it firmly in place as she made the move from her walker.

She smiled again; a genuine smile that shed a dozen years from her face and turned her wrinkles into laugh lines. There was life shimmering behind the gleaming green eyes; the only evidence of a strength of spirit that had not diminished, that refused to follow the dead-end path of her now weak and imperfect body. The gentlemen at the table smiled back;

Miss Margaret raised one brow and gave her silent welcome.

With Mrs. Johansen's arrival, the group was whole; it was *Oneness*, and they could all feel it. It was warm and satisfying, and the completeness gave each of them a greater sense of awareness, a returned sense of purpose and connection. During their time apart, they had lived lives, experienced adventures, and watched as the galaxy around them continued to spin and the universe continued to expand. All the while, through all the years, within each of the four of them, there had existed a hollow place that was not quite empty, a dark place from which emerged faint echoes of the souls of the others. The long years had passed, and they had survived those years knowing that one day, *this day*, they would be together again and whole.

Mr. Borden served the soup. They took their time. There was no rush. Mr. Borden had rented the hall for the night. They talked as they ate. There were some regrets, and more than a few boasts. Old Mason brought up Miss Margaret's little escapade in Phoenix. It had made the national news. Mrs. Johansen spoke of the grandchildren that she had helped raise after her son had been killed.

Mostly, though, they talked about how it felt to be back together again.

As Mr. Borden cleared away the bowls, Miss Margaret brought coffee in from the kitchen. They relaxed and talked about their plans for the future. Some of the plans were small, some grandiose. There was a building excitement in the air. They would miss one another, as they always did, and that feeling of being apart from one another would lie within them, as it always did; but there was little to be done about that. It was the way of things.

Then it was time.

Little by little, those around the table grew quiet; a heavy somberness lay over the room. Mr. Borden took Mrs. Johansen's left hand; Old Mason took her right. Across the table, Miss Margaret sat tall, with her back straight, her eyes closed and hands gripping tightly to the gentlemen on either side of her.

Mrs. Johansen closed her eyes and slowly lowered her head until her chin rested on her chest. Numbness rose up from somewhere deep within her, spreading out, reaching out to her legs and feet, to her arms and hands, gripping at her fingers as she gripped the fingers of Mr. Borden and Old Mason. She felt a pressure in her heart as she shared her energy with her companions in the circle. The energy of the others rushed back to her, washed over her, plunged into her and pushed the air from her lungs. She threw back her head and gasped suddenly, desperately.

They were One. They were beyond the circle. They were beyond the room, and then beyond the building. They swam the clouds that darkened the evening; they caressed the mountain peaks that rose up around the town; they danced across the stars that were just beginning to show themselves. They were free for the first time in decades and they permitted themselves these few moments to explore the emotions of their release; taking in the world, taking in the space beyond it, absorbing the sensations they were allowed to feel only twice each century.

Then they set about to business.

They began the search.

They found a group of scouts on a camping trip, sitting around a fire and telling tepid ghost stories. They cautiously reached inside each of them, one by one, delicately touching at their life force, delicately caressing the energy surrounding the core of their souls.

They took a day of life from each of them. They took two days from the scoutmaster.

A young man slept in front of his television. He was dreaming that he had won the lottery and was accepting the first check. They took a week of his life. He would die a week sooner, but he would never notice.

They found a lonely old woman who had slipped on the floor in her kitchen as she had been washing her plate and cup at the sink. There was no one to help her. They took her last day.

A man sat hidden away in an alley, huddled beside a dumpster that smelled of rotting lettuce and tomatoes. He was 34 years old, but looked 60. As they took a year from him, he fell back and hit his head. He now had six months left to him and he would spend it in a drunken stupor, stumbling about in abandoned buildings and dirty alleys.

They drew two years of life from a newborn as she drew in her first breath. She would die when she was 74 instead of 76.

They took the last breath of a police officer who had been gunned down on a domestic call.

From a young couple in the throes of passion they took a year each.

A woman, much too young to be a grandmother, lost two months as she watched her young daughter giving birth to her grandson.

They took a week from another woman as she carried her groceries out to her car, exhausted after a long day that had hours yet to go.

Finding a baby that would die in three years, they did not know from what, they took it all. When the proud young parents looked in on the child moments later, their lives came crashing down around them, lives that would not be shortened, lives that would be filled with years of doubt and guilt and grief.

Shadows scurried about in the night. Seconds passed to minutes, and the minutes to hours. They fed throughout the long night, snatching away precious moments of warm existence from the flickering lights of souls lying within every spirit they came upon. As the night slipped into those empty hours before dawn and

they finished the feeding, the
searchers sought again the circle.

The room was there, the table, the
four companions with eyes now
empty and without color. The bodies
were old and weathered; the bones
fragile and muscles worn from long
decades of use.

That which had become One now
returned to the circle. Slowly, with a
sense of trepidation and loss, the One
again become four. That which was
Mrs. Johansen again realized a sense of
self, a sense of individual identity.
There was a brief moment of
heartrending anguish as she was again
the old woman.

She screamed in pain as an
explosion of life energy burst from a
tiny core within her and struck out to
every cell of her body, every fiber of
her being. It reached into her brain,
into her heart, into her ancient soul,
and swept through her decrepit form
like fire—burning, scrubbing away the
years a second at a time.

The eternal companions remained locked hand in hand throughout what remained of the night.

In the morning, young Mason brought fresh clothes out from the closet. Josie and Maggie went into the women's restroom to clean up and dress as Mason and Bill did the same in the men's restroom. The four of them lingered over a large breakfast of eggs, ham and toast, knowing that once they left, it would be another fifty years before they saw each other again.

Josie brushed back her thick, dark hair and smiled broadly at the others. The life and soul hidden away behind her gleaming green eyes showed a strength of spirit that would not diminish with time. The young men at the table smiled back; Maggie raised one brow, offered a slight smile in return. Then it was time for them to leave.

~ end

Last Day at Sharp Park

Introduction

In 1962, when I was a little boy, five or six years old, my mom moved us into a rundown converted motel that sat just off a dismal gray beach in one of those small towns south of San Francisco.

My great grandmother stayed with us for a brief time. I don't remember the exact circumstances, but I think she was caring for me while my mother was at work. Mom moved us around a lot back then.

I have several snapshot memories of our time at that ugly motel on that lonely stretch of beach. One is of a day I got off the school bus and found my grandma waiting for me on the bench that faced the ocean. Instead of going inside, we went for a long walk. It was gray and very foggy. I had the feeling that something was wrong, but she never said what that might be. We just walked along the beach, the sound of the waves coming to us through the fog. To this day I remember the stench of rotting seaweed hanging heavy in the salt-laden air.

A number of years later, when I was about 15 years old, I wrote a story about that day. Being that I often see things rather differently than you humans, there may be some slight otherworldly spin on what really happened back then.

Hey, it's my world; I'll make of it what I want.

So... here's a short story written in 1971 by a fifteen year old boy still haunted by that afternoon back when he was six...

Update: This story was used as the seed for a much larger, also adapted to a screenplay. Note that it served as the starting point only.

Last Day at Sharp Park

The old woman closed the door behind her and stepped off the tiny slab of concrete that served as the porch. The day was cold and wet and gray, and the damp was carried on a dull, chilling wind that seeped into her bones and pushed against her spirit and her will. She walked across the narrow strip of yard and took the wooden steps up the embankment that separated the small, weathered house from the beach and followed the walkway that led back around to the road.

She sat on the bench to wait for Davy. The bench faced the beach, but turning sideways she could look up the road and watch for the small, yellow school bus. It would stop at the intersection and the old woman's grandson would climb out and make the walk to the road's end and the cluster of tiny houses.

The six houses, converted from an old motel, were grouped together on the north side of the narrow road where the road emptied into a little parking lot. The houses were protected from high tides by an eight-foot high manmade embankment that took away whatever ocean view there might once have been. The south side of the narrow road bordered the back of a golf course that ran up the beach for half a mile before turning inland. The bench the old woman sat on was one of several that lined the parking lot that butted up against the beach. The lot was really just the end of the road, widened out enough to allow the few tenants a place to park, and with a little extra room for the occasional beachcomber.

This wasn't one of the more popular beaches. It was off the main tourist routes, not readily accessible, and wasn't particularly inviting. The old woman shifted uncomfortably and looked up the beach.

On top of everything else, it wasn't a very inviting day. The fog was rolling in, turning a cold, damp afternoon even more miserable. She would be glad to get Davy away from here.

There was a time when she had actually liked this place. The sound of the waves, the haunting cry of the birds, the smells born on the sea winds, the brush of the fog on her face and the sensation of sand grinding beneath her feet. She closed her eyes and tried to bring back some of what she must have felt during those first months after arriving.

She meditated; she could hear the hollow roar of the ocean, the lapping sound of the waves, and the screeching of one lonely gull. But these were with them always, were a constant part of their existence, and had become the background noise that dulled all other sounds.

The smells overwhelmed; rotting seaweed, waterlogged debris, thick gray sand that never dried, and the pungent salty reek that dominated everything.

The old woman gave up and opened her eyes. She was probably looking for something that had never really existed to begin with. She turned about to look again at the group of ugly little houses. The fog was growing thicker and the windows of several of the homes had a fuzzy yellow glow. The windows of the nearest house, out of which she had come, were a dull black. She stared at the narrow, faded door.

What a hideous little hovel. It was damp, dark, and smelly with age and an immoral past.

The sound of the school bus stopping at the intersection startled her. She stood and stepped around the bench, rested a hand on it and waited. The fog had grown so thick that she couldn't see it, but the sound of it, and the flashing lights, told her that the bus was there. She heard it pull away. It was some time before she saw the silhouette of a little boy set against the heavy gray mist.

Such a small, vulnerable child; the old woman nearly burst into tears at the sight of him. He was so thin, with wild, light brown hair bleached almost yellow from the sun. He walked awkwardly now, absentmindedly, occasionally glancing at the golf course where the fog sometimes twisted about into strange shapes across the gently rolling slopes. Today, however, it simply rolled over the wet grass and turned everything to shades of gray.

The boy caught sight of the old woman and his face brightened and he ran to her, calling out to her. He threw his arms around her and they hugged. She kissed the top of his head, then turned his head up and kissed his forehead and his cheeks and his nose and gave him a big, grandma kiss on the mouth. She hugged him again, squeezed him to her, then told him they should take a walk along the beach. She told him that she loved walks on the beach.

Davy followed beside her, glancing back once at his house. The windows were dark.

Where was everybody?

They strolled out to where the sand was wet, then turned and began walking up the beach. The fog was now so thick that Davy couldn't see beyond his hands when he held them out in front of him, couldn't see the ocean that was right beside him.

His grandma took his hand and they walked slowly. They were quiet at first, listening to the waves and the roar of the sea. The foam sometimes reached their feet. Grandma didn't seem to mind. Looking up at her, Davy could just make out her face. She was holding it up against the breeze. He turned his own face to the wind now, and felt the dampness against his skin, took in the salt smell and breathed in the wet air.

Davy liked this beach. The outside didn't come here. People didn't come here, like they did other beaches. The only sounds were the ocean's sounds. The only footprints were his footprints. There was the ocean and the sea gulls and him. He liked that.

"Davy," Grandma said suddenly. "We have to leave here soon."

"Where are we going?" Davy felt a twinge of anxiety. He looked back over his shoulder, back towards his house, but it was lost in the mist. "Where's Mommy?"

"Don't worry, sweetie," said Grandma. "Everything is going to be fine."

"Grandma? Where's Mommy?"

Grandma was solemn, silent.

"Grandma?"

"They've found us, honey. We have to leave here."

"Who found us, Grandma?"

Grandma was walking a little faster now, holding tightly to her grandson's hand. Davy, with his tiny, six year old legs, was almost running to keep up.

"Where's Mommy, Grandma?"

"You're going to have to think very clearly now, Davy. You have to be very strong and you have to think very clearly."

Davy had no idea what Grandma was talking about.

"I will, Grandma."

Grandma stopped, pulling Davy up short. She knelt, turned the boy around to face her. "You are going to have to think back now. All right? I need for you to think back to when we first came here. Do you remember when we came to this beach? To this house?"

Of course he remembered. Davy nodded.

"Do you, sweetie? Think very hard."

"Yes." Davy remembered. He and Grandma. And Mommy. And Nicolas and Ben. Nicolas was four, and Ben was three. But not when they moved here. Ben was a baby when they first moved here. Davy wasn't going to school, then. Not yet. He was too young then.

"Do you remember why we came here?"

Davy grew cold. Something was happening in his head.

"Think, Davy."

Davy stared at Grandma. Slowly then, he nodded.

Yes. I remember...

"They're after me. Aren't they, Grandma?"

"That's right, honey." Grandma's face was very stern, but her eyes were soft and warm. Behind her, the rolling fog thinned for a moment and Davy could see the ocean. Then it was gone and the two of them were swallowed up in the cold, wet mist. "Do you remember who is after you?"

"Yes," Davy said flatly.

Grandma took a deep breath and stood. It was returning to him now, after being locked away for three years. Still fragmented, but it would soon come together. She took his hand and they began walking again. The little boy's fingers, so tiny and fragile within her own, were clenching and unclenching, making a little fist inside her palm.

What a terrible, terrible thing she was doing, destroying this little boy's make-believe world. But it was necessary. He had to survive. To survive, he must leave this place.

"We're not going back home?" asked Davy.

"Back to the house? No, Davy. It isn't safe."

"What about my stuff?"

"There is nothing there," Grandma said coldly.

Davy almost stumbled, perplexed. Of course there was. His room was full of stuff. He had his desk, and his shelf full of books, and his dresser full of clothes, and the closet with all his shirts, and the boxes of stuff on the closet shelf, and the toys in the box, and the three games that he kept under his bed. And what about the TV in the living room? And the PlayStation? And the five PlayStation games?

"We have to get Mommy," said Davy.

Grandma stiffened, but kept walking. "No, honey."

"We have to get Mommy, and Nicolas and Ben."

"No, honey."

"But—" Davy was getting dizzy; dizzy and confused.

"There is no reason to go back to the house."

Davy started to cry, but he kept walking.

There was only one small bed in his bedroom...

The games under the bed he would sometimes play with Grandma, but usually he played by himself...

There was only one other bedroom in the house, and that was where Grandma slept...

Grandma picked up little Davy and squeezed him tightly as she walked on. She could feel Davy's sobs as he buried his face in her shoulder. She brushed at his hair with her free hand, and then she too began to cry.

"I want Mommy," he mumbled.

"I know, sweetie." She had to get him away. She had to get him off-planet before they came. With enough of a head start, perhaps it would take another three years to track them down again. The galaxy was a big place, with a million habitable worlds. The Emperor had only so many ships and so many warriors to spare, especially since the horrible war had begun...

When my son murdered his wife and children... all but DahVee—I got little DahVee away...

"Grandma," cried Davy. "I want to go home."

"Me too, Davy." She knew now that he was fully back. He meant *Home*. "I wish we could."

But, of course they could not. Not while Davy's father was still alive.

"Someday," she said, as they vanished into the fog. "Someday, we'll go home."

~ end

The Light in the Mist

Introduction

Another story born out of a creative writing class. One week, the assignment was to come up with a short story in the vein of a fairy tale. I went out and bought a collection of "Victorian Fairie Tales". So, Victorian it was. I didn't know there was a difference.

That was the influence. Okay, okay... maybe the Victorian Fairie Tale thing ended up as little more than a jumping off point and I went wherever this story ended up taking me. Hey, I got an A out of it...

The Light in the Mist

Galmack gripped the arm of the heavy chair and glared down at the two pathetic creatures kneeling before him. His black claws scratched across the scarred, well-worn wood of the throne arm, instinctively seeking the deep grooves formed there by centuries of his habitual attention. The two shadowy servants sensed his rising anger and threw themselves face down onto the steps at his hooved feet, spread their arms wide and began to whimper.

Galmack smiled unpleasantly. A thin line of spittle ran from the corner of his wide mouth and down his long, pointed chin. A growl began from somewhere deep within his massive, barreled chest and rolled out of him, filling all parts of the dank hall. The guards standing at the door shifted nervously. As the sound faded, Galmack leaned back and let his large, horned head rest against the back of the throne.

"A lack of sincerity," Galmack hissed. There was heat in his whisper, and the two lying prostrate at his feet felt the leathery skin on their backs begin to burn. If they lived beyond this day, there would be much pain, yet but for the barely perceptible twitching of their stubby tails, they did not move. They did not speak.

Their master sighed sorrowfully. The timber in the walls of the great room trembled. He closed his eyes and grew thoughtful.

Galmack's periodic outbursts were necessary, of course, but he tended toward such *unplanned* occurrences when those before him were well beyond breeding age. He could little afford to destroy servants indiscriminately. These two were young, just entering their breeding years. A pity...

His anger rose up within him again, coming up hot in his throat, more because he could not bring himself to kill them than for their ineptitude. His world was growing smaller, and because of that he was forced to endure the very incompetence that was the cause of all his woes.

He stood and took the two steps down to the creatures. Their fear washed over Galmack, warming him, feeding him. His hands reached out involuntarily.

How pleasant it would be. He had only to take their tiny skulls, one in each hand, and squeeze...

Daniel wed his childhood sweetheart and together they moved to the small valley far to the east of the village. They built a three-room house on the northern hillside, and they made this their home. From the doorstep, they could watch the seasons change; the summers were never too hot or too dry, the winters never too harsh. In the spring, the grasses and the trees were all shades of green, the flowers yellow and white and blue. The autumn saw the trees turn orange and brown and red. The man and his wife were happy.

Daniel worked with wood, which he skillfully shaped into the figures of the animals that he saw in the valley. Hanna worked with clay, which she shaped into pots and plates and bowls. On these she painted the images of the flowers that she saw in the meadow below their modest home. The carvings and the pots and plates and bowls they would take to the village and sell at the market. In this way they earned enough for their needs.

Late one Autumn, the man and the woman had a daughter. Sarah was sweet and happy and was a part of the valley. As soon as she was old enough, her days were spent at play outside the front door of their home on the hillside. By her sixth year, the entire valley was her playground; the daylight hours were spent in the woods, the meadow, the grassy slopes, and along the several brooks that meandered through the valley. She made friends with the deer and the rabbits and all the creatures that made the valley their home.

Also living in the valley but seldom seen were the Fairies of the waterfall. When she sat on a particular rock along the left side of the waterfall, and when the sun was just above the trees on the clearest of mornings, Sarah could see the Fairies as they played in the mist. The soft falls would dance and sparkle with life, occasionally reaching out to caress the cheek of the little girl. At this she would laugh, and hold her face against the cool mist and reach her hands into the water. She could sense the purity in the spirits of the Fairies, could feel the joy in their hearts, and now and then she could hear their voices as they laughed and sang.

Sarah was almost ten when a great darkness fell over the valley. It came on a day early in the spring, as she sat on her special rock in the bright, midmorning sun. A shadow fell across the falls and chased the Fairies deep into the water. Sarah turned and looked up at the sky.

There was something not right with this gray.

It was nothing that she could put into words, but she could feel it; there was something very wrong. She knew it. There was something there, something that did not belong, something that did not belong in the valley. There was something that did not belong anywhere. She stood, shivering in the sudden dankness of this strange world that threatened to envelope her. A slate-gray chill began burrowing its way into her. She turned and ran from the waterfall, and by the time she was home, little Sarah was crying.

With the Darkness came gray skies and clouds near black, and rains that lasted for weeks on end. With the Darkness came the swamps and the muddy bogs. With the Darkness, the grasses withered and the wildflowers died, the woods turned barren, the brooks swelled and muddied.

The home of the man and the woman and the little girl was as damp and gloomy as the unending season of gray that held the valley. It was difficult for Daniel to find wood dry enough to burn to keep them warm. He could find no wood suitable for carving. Hanna could find no clay suitable for making pots and plates and bowls. With nothing to trade, there was nothing with which to earn their keep. When their food ran out, the family lived on what they could find in the valley or managed to grow in the saturated earth of their small garden.

Spring left and summer came, and still the skies did not clear. There were no dry days. The gray was the gray that pulled down the soul, that dragged at the spirit and the heart. It grew more difficult each day for Daniel to force himself out of the house to search for food and kindling. Each day, it was the sight of little Sarah, sad and cold and hungry, that sent him out. Each day, he returned with little to eat and he was all the more weary for the day spent in search of what little could be found.

During these wanderings, Daniel would sometimes come upon the waterfall where his daughter had spent so many hours in better times. When finding himself there, he would often stop to rest, sometimes for several hours. He would sit on Sarah's special rock and watch the water work its way down the craggy hillside. Its magic no longer showed itself, but Daniel could feel a purity within the falls and it seemed to him the mist would sometimes wash just a little of the darkness from his heart and allow him to continue for one more day.

Sarah never came to the waterfall; not since the coming of the Darkness. She seldom left the house, and then went only as far as the garden. There she would toil in the muddy earth, digging for the few carrots and potatoes they managed to grow.

The summer was two-thirds gone and there was no sign that the gray was going to leave. Daniel had traveled to the far end of the valley this day and was on his way back to Hanna and little Sarah when he decided to stop again at the waterfall. It was late, but it wasn't far out of the way, and a few moments there would return him home in better spirits.

As he neared the falls, Daniel heard sounds—animal sounds, but unlike anything that he had heard before in the valley. These were sounds unfamiliar and yet known, for these were the sounds of a little boy's night terrors.

He approached cautiously, haunted by the stories that he had heard as a child and the visions those stories had left behind.

There they were—at his little girl's waterfall. Galmack's creatures.

He is here...

Daniel watched from his hiding place as the servants of Galmack scrambled across and about the falls, searching, searching... squealing grotesquely as they groped beneath the water with their bony-fingered hands and pulled out the terrified Fairies one by one, stuffing them into large bags as black as the dark, empty eyes of the evil creatures that held them. The goblins shrieked with joy each time they had one of the little Fairies in hand, crying out in fear. The little sparks of life would squirm and struggle, fighting to get away, occasionally breaking loose and rushing back into the water. More often they did not get away and were stuffed into the black bags.

The gray sky gave way to full night before the creatures were through. There were no more Fairies in the waterfall. The goblins scurried away, eager to be far from the water and more eager yet to return their newly acquired treasure to their Lord.

Not until they were long out of sight and hearing did Daniel dare to come out of hiding and rush home.

"What will we do?" asked Hanna. "We'll have to leave the valley."

"We can't stay here," Daniel agreed. It was late in the night, but they had not yet gone to bed. They could not sleep. They sat at the small table, a single candle flickering between them.

Hanna and little Sarah had been worried when Daniel had not returned home by nightfall. They were relieved to see him, only to be troubled once again when he told them of what he had witnessed at the waterfall. Sarah began to cry and wanted to hurry back to the waterfall. Daniel held her in his arms until the sobbing stopped. Together then, Daniel and Hanna told their daughter of Galmack, the evil king of a lost and wicked race, long ago driven from this land and thought forever gone. He could not live in the world of bright sunshine and was repulsed by kindness and good. He could only exist in the gray gloom and thrived on all that was bad, fed on sadness and fear.

Now he had returned, and was reshaping this valley to be his home, coloring it to his need for shadow and dark.

With thoughts and images such as these, Sarah had fallen silent before the faint warmth of the fireplace, staring into the glow of the small fire that Daniel had managed to keep going. She had finally fallen into a fitful sleep and Daniel carried her to bed.

They would have to leave the valley. Perhaps they would move back to the village. Perhaps they would find another valley. Wherever they went, it would not be home. It would not be here.

Galmack has taken our valley from us.

In the morning, Daniel woke to a scratching knock on their door. When he opened it, he saw three small, ugly creatures standing on the front stoop. They were a third his height, naked and damp, with frog-like features not unlike the things that he had seen at the waterfall the day before.

More of Galmack's servants...

Daniel reached quickly for the wooden staff that he kept beside the door.

"Away, you!" He held the staff before him.

The creatures backed away quickly, out of reach of the long staff and several paces beyond. The man came outside the house, emboldened now, out into the open and where he could fight if need be, and held his weapon at the ready.

"Let my family be!"

At this, one of the three stepped forward and spoke. It was not in any language that Daniel could understand or had ever heard. He was taken slightly aback at the softness of the voice; it was not harsh or wicked or threatening, but rather gentle and kind. Nor were the words in any way ugly, despite the hideous appearance of the creature that spoke them. When it had finished its few short sentences, the thing stepped back, and its companions nodded urgently, their heavy heads bobbing up and down with some sense of desperation.

Maybe these weren't servants of Galmack, then, but more of his victims.

"I can't help you," he said. "Leave us alone." What was he supposed to do for them? He couldn't help them; he could barely keep his own family alive. Besides, he was soon going to take his family out of the valley.

The creatures didn't leave. They stood, heads now still, and watched the man as he slowly lowered the staff to his side. They made no effort to come nearer, yet showed no inclination to return whence they had come.

"Please," Daniel pleaded, "we can do nothing for you. I can offer you neither protection, nor food. We grow hungry ourselves. What little food we would give to you would come from the mouth of my little Sarah. This I will not do."

At that last, all three of the creatures jumped forward, speaking hurriedly, frantically, desperately. Daniel quickly brought his staff again to bear, certain that they were about to attack, that something he had said had either offended them or in some other way angered them.

"Go! Go! Leave us!" He pushed his staff forward, in the direction of the creatures, to show that he meant what he said to be done.

It was several moments more before the three were able to regain their calm. A sadness hovered about them now, strong enough that the man could feel it. He knew that he could not give in to it, that if he showed any further sign of weakness, he would never get them to leave.

He stood his ground. "Leave now," he demanded.

With this they turned about and started slowly along the muddy path that led down the hillside from the house. Daniel watched them until they

were out of sight, then turned and
went into the house.

Hanna waited for him there, having
watched it all from the window beside
the door. Daniel returned the staff to
its place and put his arms around his
wife. As he held her, their daughter
came into the room and stood sleepily
before them.

"Where are the Fairies?" she asked.

"These were not Fairies," said
Daniel.

"I heard them."

The mother knelt before little Sarah,
gave her a hug, brushed back her hair
and kissed her forehead. "You were
having a dream, Sarah."

"I was awake. I heard them."

Hanna stood and turned to her
husband. Daniel shook his head
uncertainly. He knew that no one
could speak the language of the
Fairies, but he knew also that his
daughter had a special relationship
with them, that she could sometimes
hear them and understand them; not
just with her ears but with her heart.

What if these three creatures were Fairies, thought Daniel, but somehow bedeviled?

"Did you understand what they were trying to say?" he asked.

She nodded. "Something bad has been done to them."

"Yes?"

"They want me to help them."

"What would they have you do, Sarah," asked Hanna doubtfully, "that Fairies could not do for themselves?"

"I do not know," Sarah said. Her voice was quivering. She was coming full awake now, and the realization of what was happening was descending upon her. When she spoke again, the words did not sound like the words of a little girl. It was still Sarah, their sweet daughter, but she now carried a knowledge and a burden far beyond her ten years. "A spell has been laid upon them, but it is not yet finished. When it is, the darkness that has fallen upon our valley will be here forever."

"Sarah?" Hanna was growing frightened, not just for the valley, but for her little girl. "You can stop this?"

"They want me to release them from the spell before it is completed; and then the darkness on the valley will also be gone."

Daniel knew it all to be true; this and more. He could take Sarah's words and place them beside what he knew of Galmack...

Galmack had placed a curse upon three of the Fairies that he had taken from the waterfall. Yes. It would be like Galmack to make the spell all the more cruel by offering them an escape from their affliction. They had come here for help. Daniel had turned them away, as Galmack must have known he would.

Daniel held his daughter in his arms. "I'll find them," he said. "I will bring them back." He put on his hat and coat, took his staff in hand, and left.

He returned that evening, cold and hungry and alone. He emptied his pockets of the few nuts and berries and roots that he had found while searching for the Fairies. As they ate he told him of his day. He had searched the hillside, the barren woods, the swampy meadows, the brooks, and the waterfall. There had been no sign of them. The rains had washed away what tracks they may have left behind. He would go out again tomorrow.

Daniel searched for the Fairies all the next day, and the next, and the day after that. Hanna looked for them as well, and Sarah searched all the places she thought they might be. All the while, the Darkness that lay over the valley grew stronger and heavier. There was less and less to eat, and the man, the woman and the little girl grew pale and thin and weak. Eventually, all of what little food that was found was given to Sarah. Most days, Daniel and Hanna did without.

By the beginning of autumn, Hanna was too weak to leave the house. It was too much for her even to get out of bed. Daniel and their little Sarah continued to look for the Fairies.

Then, one morning, Daniel woke and found that he also was too weak to get out of bed.

Sarah continued on alone. Almost too feeble now to travel the winding path, she returned to the waterfall. She often came here first, early in the morning, before beginning her day's search. She would sit and watch the darkened water, remembering the way it was in happier times, the way it would sparkle with Fairie life, the way it would reach out to her and touch her cheek and make her laugh.

On this day she sat on her special rock, as always, along the left side of the falls, wrapped her arms around her knees, and stared into the water as it splashed down the rocks and into the small pool below. As always now, the day was gray and wet, and left Sarah chilled in spirit and body. There was little left in the falls now to wash away the growing darkness that surrounded her heart. She rested her head on her knees. She felt a tingling inside her as the falls struggled to cleanse her, to restore some sense of light and hope to her. That faded away, and then there was nothing.

Sarah reached a hand out and touched the water, too weak to do much else. She would not be leaving here again. Her last day would be spent beside the waterfall that had been the greatest joy of her life. She began to cry. Her tears ran down her cheeks and onto the wet rock.

In the gray surrounding the waterfall, a faint shimmer shown in the mist above the rock upon which her tears had fallen. It was barely visible, and it looked to fade into and out of existence. After several moments, the gentle sparkling of light spread up to wash across the little girl's wet cheeks.

This appeared to Sarah as the memories of joys forever lost, and she continued to weep. The shimmering light, still so faint that it could barely be seen, danced in the mist, reaching out toward the falls themselves. For a moment, Sarah thought she saw something, and she raised her head enough to look more closely. The image vanished.

The mist grew steadily brighter.

There it is again.

Sarah began sobbing silently, for hidden there deep within the waterfall, just visible, were three hideous little creatures. Three ugly, piteous little beings sat on a ledge within the waterfall, clutching to each other and looking despondently out beyond the falls.

She sobbed openly, now. She had found them. At last, she had found them, but she was too near death to help them. Sarah carefully laid down upon the rock, reaching a shaky hand out in the direction of the falls.

She closed her eyes and surrendered to sleep.

From within the waterfall, the creatures saw Sarah lying on her special rock and realized that she had seen them. They also began to weep.

They wept with joy, for though they too were near death and were too weak to move beyond the ledge, their Sarah had come looking for them. They held to each other all the more tightly, and also closed their eyes.

Their tears reached the pool below and rose again with the mist. The mist swelled and rose higher, until it found the little girl, her face damp with her own final tears, tears that she had shed for the three Fairies held within the spell. The mist reached out and caressed Sarah's face. The water glimmered and sparkled, and the shimmering light began to spread, brighter now. Sarah's eyes opened, and she now found that she had enough strength to sit up, though slowly. She watched as the light within the mist and the water reached into the falls and touched the three creatures hidden within. Their eyes opened. Still holding one another, they stood up unsteadily and let the water rush over them. The falls ran clearer and brighter; the three creatures began to shimmer as well, then paled to bright, misty orbs.

Sarah began to laugh. She held her hands out before her to let the bright, clear water run through her fingers. Her face glowed with the cool, wet mist and the tears that ran freely down her cheeks.

The sky directly overhead began to clear, turning a pale blue, then a deep, bright blue. The sun shone through and the woods around the waterfall were suddenly streaked with bright yellow sunlight. The air around the waterfall began to sparkle with the dancing light of Fairies.

The others were returning home, rushing home, freed now from their imprisonment by the servants of Galmack. They darted about the falls, into the mist and out, circling around Sarah, around and around, singing out their joy and their affection. Sarah laughed and sang with them. She sat there on the rock, smiling and giggling, too weak to stand or walk. One by one, the Fairies came to her, kissed her lightly on the cheek, and entered the waterfall. When the last had returned, the waterfall of the Fairies sparkled as clear and bright as it had before the coming of the great Darkness.

The shimmering light of the waterfall reached out across the valley. It reached the home of Daniel and Hanna and little Sarah. It reached further, beyond the valley, to the great hall deep in the mountain that was the dark lair of Galmack. He roared out in anger and the mountain shook. The great thunderclap shattered across the sky and cleared away the last of darkness.

Daniel found Sarah asleep on the rock beside the waterfall. He carefully lifted her in his arms, carried her home and put her to bed. There she slept until late the next morning, dreaming of warm sunshine, wildflowers and Fairies.

~ end

Room

Introduction

At the end of class late one Tuesday evening, our creative writing teacher gave us an assignment that was to be handed in on Thursday. We were to write a "white room" story. This is one in which there is usually only a single, minimal set, very few if any objects, and the characters interact primarily with one another.

I had been mulling over a scene in my mind for a larger story I was thinking about writing (never did), and I thought it might fit the requirements for the assignment. Since we only had two days, I decided to go with it. In the end, it came fairly close to what the teacher wanted, though there were a few things in the room (unseen overhead light, door, walls), and I did cut away to another set and set of characters at one point. It was well received in class, and I did get another A out of it.

I ran across the story years later, along with my notes for the novel I had been thinking about at the time. You have a read and you tell me whether or not this looks more like a scene from a low-budget sci-fi B movie...

Room

The door closed slowly behind him, coming to rest in its jamb with a heavy, hollow sound. The darkness swept up and enveloped him, washed over him, and gripped at his chest. He stood motionless, clutching at the cloth bag that held the few possessions they had allowed him.

Paul Mendel sensed that he was not alone, and after a few moments he thought that he could hear breathing. The soft sound came from no direction in particular and from all directions at once. He waited, and as his eyes adjusted there was a lessening of the dark some distance directly ahead of him. He stepped towards it.

The sounds remained unchanged. He walked slowly, and as he drew nearer, Paul could see a circle of light some ten feet across forming a luminescent, ethereal cylinder of light that spanned floor to ceiling. A few more steps and he was standing at its edge, the gray coveralls and the open-toed sandals that he wore glowing faintly.

He stepped into the light, and when nothing happened he let out a long breath and moved into the center of the circle. Above him, the light shimmered as an indistinct haze. Around him, the world beyond the circle was a great, black shadow reaching into the unknown; a shadow that held the faint sounds of life, though what that life was he did not yet know.

"It's not as empty as it feels." It was a woman's voice, coming from somewhere in the dark. She was nearby but safely hidden.

"It doesn't feel empty at all," said Paul, looking in the direction of the voice. He spoke with a calmness that he didn't really feel.

"I sometimes think of it as a populated void," she said.

"You don't see many of those."

"Yeah, well, this place is full of contradictions." There was a deliberate softness to the voice, as if she was afraid the world around her might shatter if she wasn't careful. "It's intentional."

"Would you mind? I'd feel more comfortable if I could see you."

A young woman stepped into view, stopping just at the perimeter of light. She was slim in her own gray coveralls. She wore her dark hair pulled back into a long ponytail. Her hands were stuffed into her pockets. She looked to be in her twenties, and to all appearances she was a fellow prisoner. She gave a slight nod. "I'm Robin Palmer."

"Paul Mendel." There was an uncomfortable silence. "How many are we?"

"You make six."

"Quiet bunch. Where are the others?"

"Here. There is nowhere else." She turned, indicated that he should follow. "You interrupted our sleep period."

She disappeared from view. Paul had to hurry after her, following the sound of her footsteps. He allowed himself to be led away from the light, taking short, cautious, yet quick steps. Robin seemed not to be bothered at all by the fact that they were effectively blind. She knew exactly where she was going, and when she got there she came to a sudden stop.

"This is your private area," she said. "You can leave your bag here. No one will bother it."

Paul could sense a mass in front of them, but he could see nothing. Reaching out, he came into contact with a wall. It was cool, smooth, and when he ran his hand some short distance to one side, sensed a very slight inward curve.

"You'll find a mat on the floor; a blanket and pillow," said the woman.

He realized that she was about to move away, so he dropped his bag, reached out and put a hand on Robin Palmer's shoulder. She tensed slightly, but didn't pull away. After ten steps, they were back to the circle of light. Robin turned thirty degrees to the left and took Paul back into the dark. Ten more steps and she stopped.

"This is the food dispenser," she said matter-of-factly, and pulled his hand off her shoulder.

They were again at the wall, and it had the same slight curve. He realized then that the room was round. Paul found a small opening in the wall about waist high. The compartment inside was filled with soft, fleshy balls the size of large onions. Holding one to his nose, it smelled vaguely of avocado.

"Are they any good?" he asked.

"Edible," she shrugged. "We call them ration fruit, for lack of any better name. Not much flavor, I guess, but they keep us healthy. The bin is always full. You'll find a water fountain set into the wall beside the bin."

Paul heard shuffling in the dark. Some of the others were awake and moving about. This brought an important question to mind.

"Where do you go to the bathroom?"

"There's a cubicle set into the wall on the other side of the room, directly opposite us. Do you want me to show you?"

"The question was for future reference."

"Well that's it, then; the full tour."

"Do they ever turn on the lights?"

"I don't know that there are any lights."

"Except for that light in the middle of the room."

"We call that the Plaza. Central meeting place," said Robin. "As you should have figured out, the areas beyond the Plaza are for the most part divided into our private living areas. And speaking of privacy, there are two rules. You should get along fine with the rest of us if you follow them. Rule one: Keep the noise down. Rule two: When you move about, stay away from the walls. Walk to the center of the room, turn and go directly to where you need to go. This keeps you from walking through our individual quarters. If you object to either of these rules, make your objections known during a general meeting. Rules are made, changed or discarded by majority vote. It is also suggested, though not required, that you follow the schedule that has been established. Everything sound all right with you?"

"That depends on the schedule."

Robin had expected a simple affirmative. She responded to his comment calmly enough, however. "We have an eight hour sleep period and we meet for meals three times a day. We have an exercise period mid-morning, and a recreation period mid-afternoon. There is sometimes a storytelling in the evening."

"Sounds interesting."

"Yes," she said, flatly. "The Major is our clock. He's as close to a timepiece as we have in here. Not everyone gets involved in every activity, and you don't have to attend on a daily basis, but it would keep you busy. With a new arrival in town, attendance should be high at today's activities."

"If this is your sleep period, it may take me a while to get adjusted to the schedule. It's late afternoon outside."

"As I said, following the schedule is voluntary."

"I'll do my best, Miss Palmer."

Paul Mendel sat at the edge of the Plaza, his legs crossed and slowly growing numb. His five new companions sat with him, finishing their breakfast of ration fruit. Robin had introduced each of them, and each had said a few words about who they were and where they came from. They stared openly at him now, waiting for him to say something about himself. He swallowed the last of his breakfast and glanced about at the circle of faces. It was a strange mix of people.

In addition to himself and Robin Palmer, there was an army intelligence officer, a college professor, a big city police detective, and a retired government employee.

"I had a wife before the war," he began. "I had two kids. I had a house and a station wagon and a cute little sports car. Then the war came. We escaped into the mountains, and eventually joined up with the Resistance. My wife was killed a year ago, my kids not long after. Then, four

or five weeks back, we were overrun
by the Kraandar. The few of us who
survived the attack were scattered.
I've been on my own ever since. I was
captured two days ago. Here I am.
Wherever *here* is."

"Montana," said Professor Vandover.

"Northern Arizona," said Major
Mendosa.

"What line of work were you in,
son?" asked Miss Bailey. Ruth Bailey
was 62, had retired from state
government work a year before the
war broke out. In the first week of the
conflict she had lost her sister and
brother-in-law, and their kids. They
had been her family. A lot of people
knew an awful lot about losing family.

"My wife and I had an antique
furniture store," said Paul. "We looked
for items that hadn't been well cared
for. We'd get a good price, then repair
and refinish, bring them back to life,
then put 'em out front for sale."

"That's very sweet," said Miss Bailey.
"You and your wife worked together,

and at something meaningful; something with purpose."

"We liked what we did. And it provided us as much as we needed."

"How sweet," said Miss Bailey again.

"Sweet," grunted Major Mendosa. "Give us news of the war, Mr. Mendel."

"We're not making it easy for them, Major."

"What the hell does that mean?"

"I'm sorry if I sound vague, but it means just that. We're making it difficult for them to win."

"If you plan to lose, Mendel, you'll never win. Are you a loser, Mendel?" There was the look of growing distaste on the Major's face. He appeared about to spit, as if trying to rid himself of the awful flavor of something rotten that he'd just bitten into. He was clearly not much impressed with the newcomer.

"That's fine for the troops, Major," said Paul, "but I'm afraid that, barring an act of a higher power, we *will* lose. I don't like it, I'm not taking it very well, but I'm not blind to it, either."

Major Mendosa turned away from Paul in an obvious dismissal, shook his head and stared at the floor in front of him, "We couldn't get someone in here with a trained eye? Someone with the background to truly understand the situation outside?"

"Paul's assessment is probably fairly accurate," said Carl. Carl Josephsen was in his late thirties, had thick, bushy hair and a narrow face that held the look of constant contemplation. He had been a police detective before the war and had the calm air of quiet authority.

The Major growled now at Carl. "Yes, we all know your thoughts, Josephsen."

"As we all know yours, Major."

"Please," said Miss Bailey. "Must we always argue amongst ourselves?"

"Best he knows where we all stand," said the Major, though he grumbled under his breath now. Being surly with Miss Bailey apparently made him uncomfortable.

"That can be done without resorting to personal attacks, can it not?" she asked.

"Of course it can, Miss Bailey," said Professor Vandover. The professor was a tall, thin, sixtyish black man, just beginning to gray at the temples. "I believe the Major may be having difficulty restraining his frustration."

"I can speak for myself, Vandover," said Major Mendoza.

"No doubt."

The Plaza was empty but for Paul Mendel and Robin Palmer. Paul smiled and Robin shrugged uneasily.

"Lively," said Paul.

"It gets that way, sometimes," Robin said, shrugging it off. "The Major is all Army Intelligence. I think he feels cheated at having a motley group like us for a command."

"I didn't get the feeling that he was in charge."

Robin laughed, then leaned closer, "Which only adds to his distress."

This was first sign that Robin Palmer was capable of simple pleasant conversation. She was visibly different than she had been in the morning. She was more relaxed around him, now.

"I haven't heard much about you, Robin. How'd you end up in here?"

"Not much to it. I had just picked up my bachelor's, and was starting graduate studies. And the whole world turned upside down. Graduate studies were over."

"There's got to be more to it than it."

"The Professor and I were captured together."

"You and Vandover?"

"There were eight of us at his house when they took us. His wife was killed, and a couple of my friends. He and I ended up here; alone at first. A few weeks later, Miss Bailey was brought in."

Paul looked up at the ceiling, into the light. There was nothing to see but the misty glare.

"How do they treat prisoners?"

Robin shrugged, "We're on our own. The Professor says they're studying us. The Major believes it's more sinister than that."

"What do you think?"

"They're watching us. They're always watching us."

Professor Vandover was sitting alone in the Plaza when Paul came in, several ration fruit in hand.

"Hello, Professor."

"Good morning, Mr. Mendel."

"Paul. Paul is fine." Paul sat beside him. "I wish they would supply us with a few chairs."

"Furniture has been requested, but not provided."

"Yeah? How do you make requests?"

"Young Miss Palmer voices our desires in the general direction of the light above us."

Paul could swear he saw the beginnings of a smile on the Professor's face. He looked up into the light, wondering if, as Robin suggested, they were always watching.

"Does it ever work? Asking the light?"

This time Professor Vandover did manage a smile, if only for a moment. "Not as yet."

Paul held out a ration fruit to the Professor. Vandover slowly shook his head. "No thank you, Mr. Mendel. I will wait for the others."

Paul took another bite of the one that he was eating.

Paul mapped out the room over the next several days. First he calculated the length of his average step. Once he was convinced that he could rely on this average, he went to work. He paced the distance from the wall of his quarters area inward to the center of the Plaza. He did this going both directions, several times. His shortest calculation was within one and a half feet of his longest calculation. He took the average—thirty-five feet.

He performed the same process to the food dispenser, then to the toilet and shower. The distance to each, from the center of the Plaza, was thirty-five feet.

Paul wasn't much for mathematics, so he went with the clock picture. He figured that if his quarters lay at 12 o'clock, then the food dispenser was somewhere near 4 o'clock and the toilet was at 10. He did know enough math to calculate that if this was a circle, and the radius was 35 feet, then the circumference would be a little over 220 feet. He decided to test his math.

Paul waited until the others were in the Plaza. Starting from his quarters, he began a clockwise walk along the wall. He came first to Professor Vandover's quarters. He couldn't actually see anything, but he found the mat at about where he guessed it would be from the direction of the Professor's comings and goings from the Plaza, at just past the 1 on the clock.

Next was the Major's quarters, at almost 3 o'clock. At the 4, Paul found the food dispenser. He found Miss Bailey's quarters at 6 o'clock and Robin's at just past 7. Between 8 and 9, he found the solid door that he had first come through. At 10 was the toilet with the shower stall. Carl Josephsen's quarters were at 11 o'clock. Back at 12, and at about the 220 foot circumference that he had estimated, he was back at his own quarters.

The others had of course known what he was up to, and upon his return to the Plaza had voiced their objections and feigned outrage at his plodding through private quarters, but he sensed it was obligatory fury. They certainly must have expected the new arrival to explore his prison cell, and they hadn't tried to stop him during his exploration. Once he had completed his search, they had dutifully scolded him for his offense and then had dropped the matter. He would not be going through their private areas again.

Paul could not reach the top of the wall. When he asked Carl about it, he was told that some weeks back Robin had stood on his shoulders, and she had not found the top of the wall. This would put the height of the room, at the outer edge, at somewhere beyond 12 feet, perhaps much more. The light above the Plaza was certainly much higher than 12 feet.

The walls and floor felt like metal; cool but not cold to the touch. Inside the food dispenser, Paul could feel the joint that formed the small access from which the ration fruit came. Even if he could manage to pry it open, which he doubted, it was barely wide enough for his hand, just large enough for the ration fruit.

The toilet cubicle, with the overhead shower nozzle, showed nothing in the way of an opportunity.

Paul saw three areas for further research.

First, with the help of the others, he could continue to search for the ceiling. Being as out of reach as it appeared to be, perhaps it was more vulnerable, and perhaps there was a way through.

A second area of further research was the door that he had come in through. The door itself was impenetrable, but if Paul was waiting nearby when someone new was brought in, he could try and make a fight of it. He wasn't hopeful. He couldn't spend all his time waiting by the door, and if he did happen to be there when it was opened, he would be facing jailors who would no doubt be on their guard. There also remained the question as to just what to do if he did manage get past these first guards.

A third possibility was to find a way to have his captors take him out of the room of their own accord. This option, he would have to think on...

§

"Mr. Mendel?"

Paul turned at the sound. He was standing vigilantly beside the door. "Yes?"

"It's Carl Josephsen."

Paul could just sense a figure in the dark. He heard the faint sound of the police detective's sandals on the floor. Back in the middle of the room, he heard the others talking as they sat about in the Plaza.

"Call me Paul."

"I thought you might be here, Paul." Josephsen stopped. Very little of the light from the Plaza went beyond the Plaza itself, but Paul found that as time passed, his eyes grew more acute to subtle shades of dark, and as some little light did reach out from the center of the room, it was not totally black in the cell. There was light. Paul could in some sense see Josephsen standing beside him. Once he had the man's position, he turned back to the door.

"As good a place as any to idle away the time."

"Of course. Most of us have spent time here. I spent weeks here. Just waiting... I'm not sure what I would have done if the door had actually opened—probably would have jumped back and hid in the dark."

"Can you see everything in here when the light from outside shines in? Can you see the ceiling?"

"Afraid not. You can't tell when you're brought in, Paul, but the moment the door opens, the light in the hall outside goes real dim. From in here, if you're in the right place at the right time, you can make out the silhouette of someone standing in the door, but that's about it."

Paul looked up at the ceiling. It was dark everywhere, but it was darkest up there. If it was totally black anywhere, it was totally black up there.

"Has anyone actually been here at the door when it opened?" he asked.

"Not this near, no."

"Has it ever opened except to let in a new prisoner?"

"Not that I know of." Carl turned at the sound of the Major's raised voice in the Plaza. "Someone has the Major ticked off," he said lightly. Paul sensed the smile on Carl's face. He smiled in return.

"That doesn't take much doing."

"None at all," said Carl. "But then, I guess if we didn't have the Major here, we'd have to make one."

"Suppose so," said Paul. He was about to ask another question that suddenly occurred to him, when he realized that he couldn't remember what it was. It was there, right on the tip of his tongue, and then it was gone.

That's weird...

He felt a strange tingling in his stomach. He thought he heard Carl take in a sharp breath. The voices in the Plaza stopped. Silence closed in from the dark.

The moment passed. It lasted only few seconds, then Miss Bailey was chiding the Major. The Major groaned. Carl, at arm's length in the dark, breathed noisily through his nose.

"Probably right," said Paul.

"People like the Major keep the adrenaline flowing in an otherwise peaceful world." His sandals scratched across the floor, "I'm going to head back. Miss Bailey has promised a storytelling."

"I was just a young thing," said Miss Bailey. "I had been to the Spring Dance, and was on my way home. I stopped in the park and thought I'd sit in the gazebo and enjoy the warm evening for a few minutes."

Miss Bailey had a spark in her eye, as if she was telling the group of something naughty that she had done. Paul found the woman to be quite endearing.

"The gas street lamps that lined the park gave the night a strange, yellowing glow, plenty bright enough to see young Cornelius Smythe approaching." She grinned and nodded knowingly. "I could see the look in his eye beneath the brim of his hat."

Just how old is dear old Miss Bailey?

"The young man took the steps up into the gazebo as sweet as you please, tipped his hat in a gentlemanly way and asked if he might sit beside me a while."

"So what'd you say?" asked Robin with a grin.

"Why, I didn't know what to say. Sit down beside me? Unchaperoned?" Miss Bailey slowly leaned forward, grinned sheepishly, and snickered. "I said yes."

Paul wasn't quite sure at first, but as dear Miss Bailey continued her story, it became more and more evident that the tale she told came from somewhere out of the distant past, far too distant for the woman to have experienced the events herself.

What was unsettling was that she was clearly speaking as if from personal experience and that she was just as clearly expecting everyone to take her story as fact.

Maybe she was merely embellishing an actual event by wrapping it in antiquity.

Perhaps that was what expected from the storytellings. The others didn't seem bothered. They simply took the tale at face value and appreciated the diversion.

Paul wondered why it bothered him so much...

As she went on with her story, Miss Bailey seemed to fall deeper and deeper into the atmosphere of the time. Her words, her tone, the detail in clothing and objects, and the culture and social norms, all spoke of a time long before the world that Paul had come from.

He was glad when she finished her story.

The others in the group had thoroughly enjoyed it. They excitedly asked her questions and she eagerly responded. It all made sense to them. It began to make sense to him.

But it was all wrong.

The room was very large and was filled with row after row of occupied beds of cool metal... humans, all quite old, completely unaware, each being fed intravenously, each with a narrow metal band around the head.

A Kraandar was walking slowly down one of the aisles within the rows of beds. He was of the upper class, and faintly resembled a giant, very overweight grasshopper standing on its hind legs. He stopped at one of the tables and began a cursory examination of the human that was laying there, used its more dexterous upper hands to adjust the equipment.

Another Kraandar came into the room pushing a narrow gurney, upon which slept an old woman. Her thinning hair was brittle and nearly colorless, her skin pale and flaky.

The first Kraandar turned at the sound. It spoke in the sharp, brittle tone of the upper class—the words sounding as if they might shatter in the warm air. "Subject from 13C?" The question was more of a statement. "It is being moved to Room 4A."

The second Kraandar responded acknowledgement in the humble voice of its lower class status, then began to push the gurney up to the head of the fourth row.

Paul heard the door to their cell open and a moment later close. He had been standing near the ration dispenser, and there had been no way for him to get across the room in time.

He found Robin standing in the darkness with a young woman. The new arrival was dressed in the same style of overalls as every prisoner, wore the same flat sandals. She had long, thick brown hair that she wore pulled back into a ponytail.

"Paul," said Robin, sliding to one side as he approached. "This is Carol, recently arrived."

"Good morning," said Paul, and he reached out a hand. He added questioningly, "Morning?"

"Close enough," said Carol. They shook hands. "What is this place?"

"Good question." Paul turned and the three of them started back to the center of the room. "Just got here, then?"

"Yes," she said, following Robin and Paul toward the Plaza. "They brought me in today."

~ end

The Meadow

Introduction

This is a brief, contemplative look at a day in my life when I was twelve years old. It has stayed with me, and I finally decided that I needed to put it down on paper. No twists here. Just something I wanted to say. I wrote it a year or two after my grandfather passed away in the 1970s.

The Meadow

We had a clear view of the meadow below. A slight breeze carried up the scent of the grass and the tiny yellow flowers that covered the small valley. There was a shimmer of moisture on the vegetation and in the air, as the sun hadn't yet had a chance to warm away the dew. From our vantage point we could see the deer, a buck and two doe, as they worked their way casually across the valley floor, oblivious to or unconcerned about the two humans watching them from the outcropping of rock some hundred feet above them.

I was twelve years old and this was my first hunting trip. It was early morning in the Sierras, the sun just sending its rays down to the little meadow; those same rays were just beginning to warm my face. The granite rock upon which I sat, clutching my rifle, was still cool from the long, cold night. My grandfather sat beside me. He hadn't said a word in a long time, not since we had found our way out onto the ledge. We quietly watched the deer as they grazed.

Grandpa had told me about this place the night before as we sat at our campfire. It was his secret place,

where he came every year. My uncle
and my cousin, though they were with
us on the hunting trip, and were
camped with us, would not be coming
to the meadow.

It was Grandpa's special place, and
now mine...

I had been living with my
grandparents since I was five, with
only occasional trips to live with my
mother, and while there had been a
few men in my mother's life, Grandpa
was the only adult male figure in mine.
Unfortunately, up to that point we had
never really been very close. Perhaps
he didn't know how, or maybe he was
uncertain of his relationship with his
oldest grandson. Was he raising the
boy, or wasn't he? He had already
raised his own family. Was he now to
raise his daughter's?

In very subtle ways, this week was
going to change our relationship
forever.

Late the night before, I had
awakened to find my grandfather
sitting before the fire, entranced by

the flames. He turned his head at my movements, looked at me for a few seconds, then reached for the coffee pot. He poured, and held the cup out to me.

I had never had coffee before. Coffee was a grownup thing. I scrambled out of the sleeping bag and crawled up beside him, sat beside him. I stared into the fire and drank my coffee. Neither of us said a word. Grandpa and I just sat there at the campfire, in the middle of the night, and drank our coffee.

We sat now, watching the deer from the ledge above the little valley, and I could somehow sense that they were safe. There would be no killing on this trip. As it would turn out, it would be the only hunting trip that I would ever take with my grandfather. I didn't know it then, but as we sat there, taking in the sunrise and the smell of the grass and the bright yellow flowers, the feel of the morning dew in the air, the sight of the graceful animals below us, emphysema was slowly taking Grandpa away from me.

As I look back, thinking of my grandfather, I of course remember his final years, as he grew weaker and more helpless to the point where my grandmother had to take care of his every need; but first and always I remember back to when I was twelve, to our one and only hunting trip together, and the morning that we spent at his secret place.

Over the years, I've had more than a few deer in my sights, but I've never been able to pull the trigger. I finally gave up and bought a nice camera, and I still go hunting all the time. I occasionally go to the meadow, and I'll sit on the outcropping of rock and take in the early morning. I seldom see deer these days, but I can usually feel my grandfather's presence. We don't talk much, but then we never did...

~ *end*

www.ingramcontent.com/pod-product-compliance
Lightning Source LLC
Chambersburg PA
CBHW021122130626
46554CB00002B/822